D0512822

## WIN A NAUGHTY FAIRIES T-SHIRT!

Every time those Naughty Fairies
are hatching a plan they do their fairy code
where they come up with NF words...

### Niggle Flaptart
### Nicely Framed
### Nimble Fingers

Can you help the Naughty Fairies
find two more words beginning with
N.................. and F..................?

Each month we will select the best entry to win a very
special Naughty Fairies T-shirt and they will go into the
draw to have their NF idea printed in the next lot of books!

**Don't forget to include your name and address.**
Send your entry to: Naughty Fairies NF Competition,
Hodder Children's Marketing, 338 Euston Road,
London NW1 3BH.
Australian readers should write to:
Hachette Children's Books, Level 17/207 Kent Street,
Sydney, NSW 2000

Sweet
Cheat

# Lucy Mayflower

Hodder
Children's
Books

A division of Hachette Children's Books

# Special thanks to Lucy Courtenay

Created by Hodder Children's Books and Lucy Courtenay
Text and illustrations copyright © 2006 Hodder Children's Books
Illustrations created by Artful Doodlers

First published in Great Britain in 2006
by Hodder Children's Books

4

A Catalogue record for this book is available from the British Library

ISBN – 10: 0 340 91181 6
ISBN – 13: 978 0 340 91181 5

Printed and bound in Great Britain
by Bookmarque Ltd, Croydon, Surrey

The paper and board used in this paperback by Hodder Children's Books
are natural recyclable products made from wood grown in
sustainable forests. The manufacturing processes conform to the
environmental regulations of the country of origin.

Hodder Children's Books
A division of Hachette Children's Books
338 Euston Rd, London NW1 3BH

# Contents

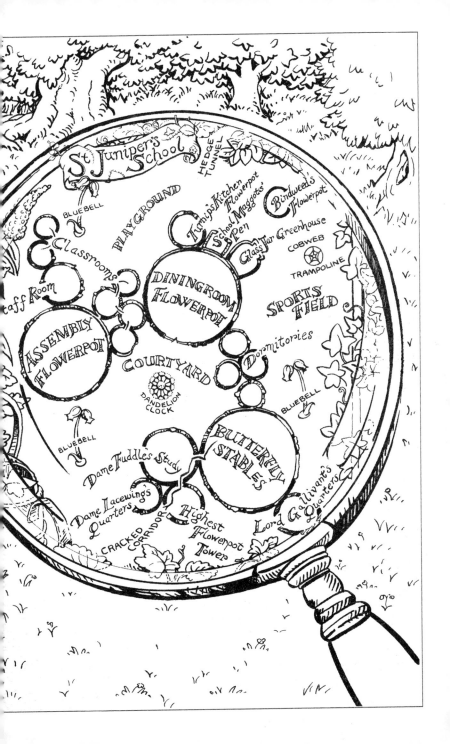

# 1

# Midnight Raid

Down at the bottom of the garden, a crescent moon hung over the fence. It was past midnight, and all the fairies at St Juniper's were asleep in their flowerpot dormitories.

Well, nearly all.

Six shadowy figures stood in the St Juniper's kitchens. A small, chubby fairy was standing on tiptoe, trying to look inside a row of hazelnut shells on the windowsill.

"What are you looking for, Tiptoe?" said the prettiest fairy in a loud voice. She had skin like chocolate and lots of curly black hair.

A blonde, short-haired fairy with two

spiders hanging from her ears waved her hands in the air. *Shut up, Brilliance!* she mimed.

"Shut up yourself, Nettle," Brilliance said. "Come on, Tiptoe. You got us out of bed for this."

*Brilliance!* mouthed an anxious-looking fairy behind Brilliance. An ant was peeping out of her pocket and sniffing the night air with interest. *Someone will hear us!*

"Maybe you're scared, Sesame," said Brilliance, "but I'm not." She glanced around the kitchen. "I'm never scared," she added.

"It's obvious what we're looking for, Brilliance," said a red-haired fairy in a stripey black and yellow dress, who was leaning against the kitchen door and looking bored. "Food."

There was a dramatic gasp. "You're sooo clever, Kelpie," said an Oriental-looking fairy. "However did you guess?"

"Since you ask, Ping," said Kelpie, "we're in a kitchen in the middle of the night, and Tiptoe's in charge. I'm guessing we're not windsurfing. Hurry up, Tiptoe. Flea'll wonder where I am."

"The only thing your bumblebee ever wonders about is his next meal," Nettle said.

Sesame glanced at Tiptoe, who was reaching up as high as she could and feeling around inside the hazelnut shells. "Sounds like someone else we know," she said.

The fairies giggled.

"Nearly there," Tiptoe panted, moving on to the next shell. It was here somewhere, she was sure of it. She could smell its sweetness somewhere very close at hand – closer . . . closer . . .

"What was that part about staying quiet again?" Kelpie asked, as a hazelnut shell clattered to the ground. Ingredients scattered across the floor, pale in the moonlight.

"We're *so* going to get a detention," Sesame moaned.

"I don't understand it," Tiptoe said in frustration. "Turnip was making some yesterday. I'm sure I smelt it."

Turnip was the St Juniper's kitchen pixie. He was large and red-faced with a very loud voice and a dangerous temper.

"Made some what?" Brilliance demanded. "Honeycakes? Mint twists?"

"Toffee," said Tiptoe.

There was a moment of silence. Turnip's toffee was worth at least two detentions. Turnip's toffee tasted of nuts and caramel and lavender all rolled up together, with an extra *something*. No one could ever work out what that *something* was. But everyone agreed that it made Turnip's toffee totally twinkle-tastic.

"Where is it?" Ping breathed.

"I can smell something over there . . . " Sesame said, pointing to a pile of tin-foil pans stacked beside the walnut-shell sink.

Tiptoe, Ping, Brilliance and Sesame all rushed across the kitchen towards the pans. Kelpie and Nettle followed more slowly behind them.

Nettle was the only one who noticed the puddle. "There's a puddle on the . . . " she began.

"Wha . . . !"

Tiptoe's foot slid through the puddle. She skidded and crashed into a cupboard with a *crump*. Ping, Brilliance and Sesame followed with a *crimp*, a *plimp* and a *prump*. The cupboard door fell open. Nutshell jars teetered dangerously on shelves. Then, with a judder, the shelves collapsed and the jars tumbled out.

"Oh – oh – oh—" Tiptoe moaned, as flour and salt and honey crystals spilled

across the floor. "Turnip is going to *kill* us!"

"I think Dame Lacewing'll do that," Kelpie said. "Look who just arrived."

A pink and green beetle was standing in the kitchen doorway, looking beadily at them. Nettle clapped her hands to her mouth. Brilliance groaned. It was Pipsqueak. Pipsqueak belonged to Dame Lacewing, St Juniper's scary Deputy Head and Fairy Maths teacher. He was fat and self-important and very, very good at telling tales.

"Nice Pipsqueak," Sesame said nervously, brushing honey crystals off her dress and standing up very slowly. "No need to tell Dame Lacewing about this, OK?"

Pipsqueak honked sharply. Then he turned and ran out of the kitchens on six stiff little legs.

"He's going to Dame Lacewing!" Tiptoe whispered in horror.

"Not now, he isn't," said Kelpie.

Brilliance had jumped on Pipsqueak's back and was trying to keep his wing cases closed tightly to his sides. Sesame rushed forward and stroked Pipsqueak's head as Ping and Nettle held the beetle's legs tightly to stop him from kicking. "Sorry, Pipsqueak," Sesame said a little helplessly. "It's for your own good."

"No, it's for ours," Kelpie said. She had found an empty leaf box and was holding it open. "Put him in here. Quick as you can!"

The fairies wrestled the struggling beetle into the leaf box and slammed the lid. Nettle's ear spiders spun enough silk to wind around the box until it was completely secure. Pipsqueak honked furiously, but the leaf box muffled the sound.

Sesame made a small breathing hole in the top of the box. She put her eye to it and peered in. Pipsqueak stared out.

"He'll be fine," Nettle reassured Sesame, as Sesame straightened up. "Beetles love boxes. Turnip'll find him in the morning."

"Along with the rest of this mess," Brilliance added, glancing at the jumbled ingredients on the floor. "We've got to get out of here, Tiptoe – with or without the toffee."

Kelpie leaned down and peeped through the leaf box's breathing hole. "If you tell Dame Lacewing anything about this tomorrow, Pipsqueak," she said in a menacing voice, "then I promise on my wand that Flea'll sting you so hard that you'll look like a pink and green balloon."

Pipsqueak's honk sounded higher than usual as Kelpie stood up again. The fairies crept out of the kitchen. Tiptoe glanced longingly over her shoulder, looking for the toffee one last

time. Then she followed the others back
to bed.

## 2

# Owning Up

"Can you see him?" Sesame whispered to Tiptoe.

It was morning, and the fairies were halfway through breakfast. Tiptoe stood up from the table and peered down the Dining Flowerpot to where the St Juniper's teachers were sitting.

Dame Fuddle, Head of St Juniper's, was staring dreamily at a book with a picture of a handsome elf on the cover.

Lord Gallivant, St Juniper's butterfly riding teacher, was plaiting his fringe.

Bindweed the garden pixie was putting clover buns in his pocket for later. Legless the school earthworm was curled several times around his feet.

Dame Honey, the Fairy English teacher, was scribbling something on her petal napkin and passing it to Dame Taffeta, who taught Fairy Science. Dame Taffeta was giggling.

Dame Lacewing was frowning, which was normal.

Tiptoe stared hard at Dame Lacewing's feet.

"Well?" demanded Brilliance.

"Pipsqueak's not there," Tiptoe said, sitting down. "Maybe Turnip didn't find him this morning. Maybe he's still in his box."

"But he'll be hungry!" Sesame said in distress.

"No he won't," Kelpie said, stroking the extremely hairy bumblebee sitting by her side with its head on her lap. "He's a beetle. He'll eat the box."

"If he'd done that, he'd be with Dame Lacewing by now," Tiptoe said, sounding anxious.

"If I'd just eaten a box," Kelpie said, "I'd go and sleep it off somewhere."

Tiptoe's face cleared. "Of course!" she said with relief, and turned her attention back to the pile of clover buns on her plate.

To her surprise, they were cold.

"These buns are like rocks," said Sesame, prodding hers.

Tiptoe glanced at Turnip. The kitchen pixie was pacing behind the food counter. He was muttering to himself and whacking his hand hard with a kitchen spoon.

There was a crack and a spark at the teachers' long bark table. All the fairies in the Dining Flowerpot turned their heads. Dame Lacewing, tall and thin and dark as a winter twig, lowered her wand briskly.

"We have several notices this morning," she said. "Firstly, Turnip came to me this morning with some grave news."

*Pipsqueak's dead*, Tiptoe thought with horror. *He suffocated to death in that box. We should have made the breathing hole bigger. We should never have . . .*

"Someone broke into the kitchens last

night," Dame Lacewing continued.
"Turnip spent over two dandelions
clearing up the mess this morning."

"I had no time to BAKE!" Turnip
roared from the food counter, making
everyone jump. "That's why ye've
yesterday's clover buns this morning.
I've no doubt ye'd all like to THANK
the fairy responsible for THAT!"

The atmosphere in the Dining
Flowerpot turned nasty. Fairies
muttered and stared at each other.
Tiptoe put down her bun. Suddenly it
looked about as appetising as a mouse
dropping.

"Thank you, Turnip," said Dame
Lacewing. "Now, if you own up to
Turnip this morning, your detentions
will only be Unpleasant. If you wait
until this afternoon, your detentions will
be Horrible. And," she added, "if you
wait until this evening . . . " She paused
and smiled grimly. "Then the May Day

Feast on Sunday will be cancelled."

There was a gasp of horror. The May Day Feast, due to take place the day after tomorrow, was one of the best events of the fairy year. There was dancing, and games, and butterfly sports, and a huge banquet. It was a very old tradition. Surely they couldn't *cancel* it?

"Everyone's looking at our table," Tiptoe said uneasily.

"Yup," said Brilliance.

"What are we going to do?" Sesame wailed, covering her eyes.

"Own up, of course," said Ping. She looked at Tiptoe. "We don't want to miss out on the May Day Feast."

"We can get the detention out of the way, and still have the May Day Feast to look forward to," Nettle added. She also looked at Tiptoe.

"I don't care," said Kelpie. "I hate the May Day Feast."

"I'll say it was me," Tiptoe whispered, feeling sick. "I won't mention any of you. It's my fault anyway, because I wanted to look for the toffee. I'll do it after breakfast."

"Good for you, Tiptoe," said Sesame, sounding relieved.

"Think of all that lovely food at the May Day Feast," Nettle encouraged.

"Just don't think about it when you're feeding the school maggots," Kelpie advised. The school maggots lived in a pen beside the kitchen. They ate the school waste and kept the bins clean.

"Oh," Tiptoe moaned.

"Finally," Dame Lacewing said, "I'm sorry to say that my beetle Pipsqueak has disappeared. Any information will be gratefully received." And she sat down abruptly.

"Has Dame Lacewing been crying?" Sesame asked in astonishment.

"Dame Lacewing never cries," Brilliance said.

"I saw her cry once," Kelpie said.

"You did?" The others stared at Kelpie with interest.

"Sure," Kelpie said. She snapped off a piece of stale clover bun and gave it to Flea. The bumblebee sniffed it and looked disgusted. "When I handed in some homework last term."

After breakfast, Tiptoe hovered

uncertainly by the teachers' table. *I've got to own up*, she told herself. *I've got to do it. I've . . .*

"Get out of my way!" Turnip roared, looming over Tiptoe with a stack of leaf plates in his arms. "I've the whole Dining Flowerpot to clear and a Fairy Cookery lesson first thing, not to mention the mess in my kitchen. When I get my hands on the fairy who did it, I'll not be responsible for my actions."

Tiptoe's knees felt weak. "Um, Mr Turnip, sir . . . "

"What is it?" Turnip barked.

"Um," Tiptoe faltered. "I . . . I . . . "

Turnip gave an exclamation of impatience and pushed past her.

"I did it," Tiptoe whispered, looking at Turnip's square, angry back as he disappeared into the kitchen.

The others were waiting for Tiptoe outside. The dandelion clock in the middle of the courtyard lost a dandelion

seed, which spiraled into the sky.

"So?" Brilliance demanded. "Did you tell him?"

Tiptoe nodded miserably.

"Well done," Ping said in an admiring voice. There were only two teachers at St Juniper's that Ping was afraid of, and Turnip was one of them.

"The trouble is, I don't think he heard me," Tiptoe mumbled.

"Plenty of time to change that,"

Kelpie said, as Flea zoomed around over her head in the bright May sunshine. "We have Fairy Cookery now."

Tiptoe felt even sicker. The last dandelion seed fell off the dandelion clock. A clump of bluebells in the corner of the courtyard started ringing. Fairy Cookery was about to begin.

# 3

# Detention

Turnip glared at the group of fairies in his kitchen.

"Ye'll excuse the mess," he said sarcastically. Fragments of nutshell pots and jars still lay on the floor. "Aprons on."

The fairies scurried to the twig pegs by the kitchen door and took down their petal aprons. Everyone was always on their best behaviour in Fairy Cookery. Turnip was terrifying.

"You have to tell him," Brilliance said to Tiptoe in a low voice as they walked over to the large bark table where Turnip had set out several nutshell mixing bowls. "The longer you leave it, the worse it'll be."

"You don't have to tell me that,"
Tiptoe muttered, smoothing her apron
with shaking hands. She glanced at the
corner where they'd left Pipsqueak in
his leaf box. There was nothing there
at all.

Turnip brought his kitchen spoon
down on the bark table with a crash.

"Violet crisps," he barked.
"Ingredients, now!"

A green-haired fairy put up her hand.
"Violets?" she suggested.

"Violets?" Turnip said incredulously.

"VIOLETS? Of course we use violets, ye useless piece of bogweed! What else?" He pointed his kitchen spoon at Sesame. "Ingredients!"

"Hot oil," Sesame stammered.

"Hot enough to take yer eyebrows off, if ye get too close," Turnip said with a nasty smile.

Several fairies felt their eyebrows surreptitiously.

"What. Else. Do. We. Need?" Turnip said, whacking the bark table between words like full stops.

There was silence. Turnip threw his spoon to the ground and picked up a nutshell. "Salt," he said in a dangerous voice, before banging the nutshell down again. He did the same with a nutshell next to it. "Rosemary." Then he picked up a tiny white flower with star-shaped petals and twirled it between his fingers. "And a sprig of snow-in-summer to stop it burning." He crushed the snow-in-summer flower in his fist and looked meaningfully at the class. "Ye have twenty dandelion seeds," he growled. "Starting NOW."

Brilliance picked up a tinfoil pan and put it on a nearby firefly to heat it up. Nettle collected the violet petals, while Sesame and Ping ground some salt and rosemary. Kelpie slopped some oil into a nutshell and carried it over to Brilliance, and Tiptoe picked up a piece of snow-in-summer.

Soon, the kitchen was full of the smell

of seething, frying violets. One group of
fairies burned their eyebrows off with
much squealing. Another group forgot
to put in the snow-in-summer, and their

tinfoil pan went up in flames. Turnip's face grew redder and redder as he prowled around the kitchen.

He stopped at the Naughty Fairies' group. "Show me what ye've got now," he demanded.

Brilliance scooped a perfectly fried violet crisp out of the oil and offered it to the Fairy Cookery teacher. Turnip took the crisp and bit into it.

"Not bad," he said after a moment. "A wee bit more salt, mind."

"Now," Ping hissed, digging Tiptoe in the ribs. "When he's in a good mood!"

"I'll not have talking," Turnip began.

In a fit of terrified bravery, Tiptoe spoke up. "About the mess in your kitchen, sir . . . It was me. I'm very sorry. I was hungry."

There was a long and awful silence. The other fairies looked round with large eyes.

"I don't feed ye enough, eh?" Turnip said after a moment. "Hmm. Ye'll meet me here after supper every night for a week, then. Agreed?" And nodding, he moved off towards another group.

The Naughty Fairies gaped at each other. Tiptoe's knees gave way and she sat down.

"That's *it*?" Brilliance asked.

"I thought he might try and boil you with the violet crisps," Kelpie added. She sounded wistful.

Nettle clapped Tiptoe on the back.

"Hey, it's over," she said kindly. "Have a violet crisp. Like Turnip said, they're not bad."

"I thought Dame Lacewing was a bit weird in Fairy Maths today," Brilliance commented, as they made their way to the Dining Flowerpot for supper. "She added up a couple of sums wrong, did you notice?"

"The sums looked all right to me," Tiptoe said.

"They would," Kelpie snorted. "You're rubbish at Fairy Maths."

"Dame Lacewing's worrying about Pipsqueak," Sesame said. "I'm worrying about him too. He must have slept off that leaf box by now, and there's still no sign of him."

They glanced at the teachers' table as they sat down with their jasmine pie. Dame Lacewing wasn't eating. She was just fiddling with her pie, pushing it

around her leaf plate. Tiptoe's heart
flipflopped with guilt.

"We should look for Pipsqueak after
supper," she said. "We can search the
courtyard, and the Sports Field, and

maybe the Nettle and Strawberry Patches if we have time. It's the least we can do."

"You can't come," Nettle pointed out. "You've got your first detention."

"I'll join you as soon as I can," Tiptoe promised, scooping up the last of her jasmine pie. "You will go, won't you?" She looked pleadingly at the others.

Brilliance's eyes gleamed. "Naughty Fairies," she said, and put her fist on the table.

"Nincompoop fritters," Ping said, and put her fist on top of Brilliance's.

"Never flamboyant," was Kelpie's contribution.

"Newt fandango," said Nettle.

"Night frump." This was Sesame.

"Right for once, Sesame!" Tiptoe said happily. Sesame looked astonished. "Nuisance forever. Good plan. Thanks, guys. The detention won't be nearly so bad if . . . "

"Pssst!" Sesame dug Tiptoe in the ribs. Turnip was looming over them with his arms folded.

"Ye'll help me clear the plates," Turnip said without preamble.

Tiptoe swallowed and nodded. She scooped up an armful of empty plates from the table and followed Turnip to the kitchen. At the kitchen door, she turned to look at her friends. They all gave her the thumbs-up.

"Ye've eaten enough tonight now, have ye?" Turnip asked suddenly in the kitchen.

Tiptoe cleared her throat, which had gone dry. "Yes, sir."

"Did ye like the jasmine pie?" Turnip asked raising his eyebrows.

"It was delicious," Tiptoe said.

Turnip grunted in a pleased kind of way. "When ye've cleared the tables, I'll have ye out the back for a fetching job," he said. "Quick, now."

Tiptoe scurried around the tables as the rest of the fairies left the Dining Flowerpot, scooping up plates and sweeping leftovers on to the floor. Two ants sniffed around her ankles and dived after the crumbs. She piled everything into the walnut-shell sinks. Then she boiled some rainwater and mixed in some soapwort until she had two sinks full of bubbles. Finally, with aching arms, Tiptoe washed everything up.

"Out the back with ye," Turnip said, when she had finished. He marched out of the back door and waited for Tiptoe to catch up.

Standing just outside the door was a large grasshopper. It had two grass baskets slung over its back.

"There's just room for ye on Caddy's back as well," Turnip said. "I need a walnut and a hazelnut from the Wood. I'm making a nut meringue for the May

Day Feast. Caddy knows where to go. Ye'll find the nuts and put them in the baskets. Then all ye have to do is stay on Caddy's back and hold on to the reins till he brings ye back here."

The sun was setting. Trying not to think about being in the Wood after dark, Tiptoe obediently climbed on to the grasshopper's back.

"Mind how ye go," said Turnip, and he smacked the grasshopper's rear. The grasshopper spread a startling pair of wings and leaped smartly up in the air, nearly knocking Tiptoe off.

Tiptoe clung tightly on to Caddy's back as the grasshopper sprang through the dark

Hedge Tunnel. Grasses brushed Tiptoe's knees, and insects zoomed across their path as they crossed the Meadow. Soon, they had reached the Wood.

Ambrosia Academy, arch rival of St Juniper's, was based on the edge of the Wood. Tiptoe really didn't want to meet any Ambrosia fairies. They were all snotty and proud and pinched extremely hard. She snuggled down on Caddy's back as the grasshopper jumped past Ambrosia Academy's mushroom turrets, and sighed with relief when they were safely past.

When they reached a small thyme-scented glade near the middle of the Wood, Caddy stopped and rubbed his

back legs together. Littered on the ground were brown hazelnuts, half-wrapped in their frilly, pale green leaves. Tiptoe rolled one of them over to Caddy. Then, with a huge effort, she picked it up and slung it in one of the baskets.

The walnuts were on the far side of the glade. These were even bigger than the hazelnuts. Tiptoe rolled a smallish walnut over to Caddy. She levered it into the other basket, where it fell with a satisfying plop. Tiptoe strapped down the basket lids and climbed back on to Caddy's back, ready to head back to St Juniper's.

Then all of a sudden, everything went wrong.

Six Ambrosia Academy fairies looked up as Tiptoe and Caddy leaped over a huge tree root and crashed into the middle of their dancing circle. With a sinking heart, Tiptoe recognised the tallest, prettiest fairy. It was Glitter, the worst Ambrosia fairy of all.

"A *Juniper!*" Glitter hissed.

"Riding a *grathhopper!*" squeaked a

tiny fairy next to her. "How comm

"Shut up, Glee," drawled a third ∟
This was Gloss, Ambrosia Academy's
best butterfly rider. "What's she's got in
those baskets?"

"She'th been *thtealing* from our
Wood!" squealed Glee, stroking a very
fat pet ladybird. "Let'th get her!"

Tiptoe dug her heels into Caddy's
side and wrenched hard on the reins.
The grasshopper bunched his back legs
and soared over the heads of the
Ambrosia fairies. With a menacing
flutter of wings, the Ambrosia fairies
gave chase.

Tiptoe moaned with fear as Caddy
leaped and dived and ducked through
the undergrowth. It was getting darker
– she could hear whirring fairy wings
all around her – they were going to
catch her – they would take her nuts
and probably steal Caddy too and she'd
never get back to St Juniper's . . .

After several heartstopping dandelion seeds, Caddy crouched behind a fat piece of moss. Over the thundering noise of her own heart, Tiptoe listened as the sound of the Ambrosia fairies faded away.

But where was she? This was a part of the Wood that Tiptoe didn't recognise. The trees overhead were so thick that there was barely any moonlight. Tiptoe could smell wet marsh mud. Tree trunks loomed around like giants.

There was a soft flittering overhead. Tiptoe nearly screamed. She flung her arms around Caddy's neck and trembled as something small and dark flew overhead. One, then two strange, soft shapes that blurred with the night.

Caddy suddenly jumped smartly out of their mossy hiding place. Tiptoe buried her head against his back as he hopped and flew between the trees. The sky grew lighter as the edge of the

Wood came into view.

Tiptoe had never been so pleased to see the Meadow in all her life.

# 4

# Ghost Stories

It was past midnight in the Naughty Fairies' dormitory, and the fairies were snuggled up in bed. No one was asleep.

"How many of those flittering things did you see, Tiptoe?" Nettle asked.

Tiptoe shuddered, and pulled her foxglove sleeping bag more tightly up to her chin. "Two," she said. "They were horrible. All soft and dark and strange."

"Talking of dark," Brilliance grumbled, "can we get some light in here? Sesame, where's that glow worm you found when we were out looking for Pipsqueak?"

Tiptoe sat up. "Really? You found a glow worm?"

"Yup," said Nettle, as Sesame pulled
a leaf box out from underneath her bed.
"No sign of Pipsqueak, though."

Sesame lifted the lid of the box. A
pale greenish light filled the room as
she carefully pulled out the glow worm
and put it on her bed.

"She's so cute!" Tiptoe breathed, as
the glow worm squeaked and snuffled
at Sesame's hand.

Sesame stroked the glow worm's head. "I know," she said fondly. "I've called her Flash."

"They have soft, dark, strange things in China," Ping intoned in a hollow voice. "They catch fairies and pull their wings off. Then, very slowly, they eat them from the toes up."

Sesame squealed.

"She's never been to China," Brilliance reminded everyone.

"So?" Ping said. "I've still heard stories."

"What do these Chinese things look like, anyway?" Nettle asked, leaning on one elbow.

"No one knows," Ping said, in the same hollow voice. "Because if you see one, you're as good as . . . DEAD!"

Tiptoe burrowed down deep in her sleeping bag. The others laughed, sounding nervous.

"Hold on to your wings!" Nettle said,

a bit hysterically. "A dark thing is coming this way!"

Tiptoe felt someone tweaking the tip of her wing. She screamed.

"Be quiet in here!"

Dame Lacewing stood silhouetted in the doorway. "It's past midnight. If I have to come in again, you'll all have detentions tomorrow." She glanced at the glow worm on Sesame's bed. "And I expect that glow worm to be back where you found her in the morning," she added.

Tiptoe saw Dame Lacewing's eyes flick down to the empty space by her ankles, where Pipsqueak usually stood. Then at last she turned and walked quietly away.

Sesame put Flash back into her leaf box and the fairies settled down. In the silence, Tiptoe tried not to think about the Chinese fairy-eater. But the more she tried, the bigger and deadlier it got.

She squeezed her eyes tightly shut and
tried to think about Turnip's toffee
instead. Then at last, she fell into an
uneasy sleep.

It was Saturday morning, and the
fairies were going on a Nature Ramble
with Dame Honey, the Fairy English
teacher. Dame Honey was everyone's
favourite teacher. She had long dark
hair, and wore bright clothes and

beautiful flower shoes.

The fairies had gathered in the Fairy Nature Studies Flowerpot while Dame Honey gave out petal pads and charcoal splinter pencils.

"Tiptoe?"

Tiptoe opened her eyes. Dame Honey was leaning over her desk. "I thought we'd lost you," Dame Honey laughed. "Come on. The others are waiting outside already."

Yawning, Tiptoe followed Dame Honey out of the flowerpot.

"Why didn't you wake me?" she whispered to Sesame, as they moved off in a straggly line across the Sports Field.

"You just looked too comfortable," Sesame confessed.

Tiptoe looked around. "So where are we going?" she asked.

"A beetle hunt," Nettle said.

Suddenly, Tiptoe was awake. "We're looking for Pipsqueak?" she asked.

Brilliance shook her head. "Just random beetles," she said.

"I hate beetles," Kelpie said gloomily, swishing at the grass with her wand. Flea buzzed through the air above her, chasing his sting round and round in wonky circles.

"You're to fly in pairs," Dame Honey said with a smile. "We're rambling deep in the Hedge this morning."

The fairies lined up, chattering and

laughing. Kelpie whistled for Flea as Dame Honey took off, and jumped on the bumblebee's back.

"Why do you never fly with your own wings, Kelpie?" Tiptoe asked, as they flew together towards the Hedge.

"Can't be bothered," said Kelpie. "Flea needs the exercise, anyway."

The fairies flew slowly into the darkness of the Hedge. Dame Fuddle was waiting for them halfway along the Hedge Tunnel, beside a rotten twig. Next to the twig was a long, slim beetle lying on its back. It waved its hairy legs pathetically.

"This is a Click Beetle," Dame Honey said, when all the fairies had gathered together.

The beetle struggled.

"Poor thing!" Sesame said. "Can't we help it up, Dame Honey?"

"Why is it called a Click Beetle?" Brilliance asked.

The beetle suddenly leaped into the air with a loud CLICK and landed on its feet. It stared at the fairies, and then scuttled away into the Hedge.

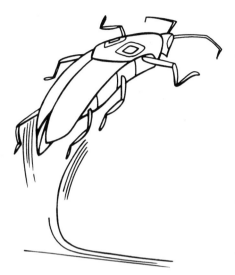

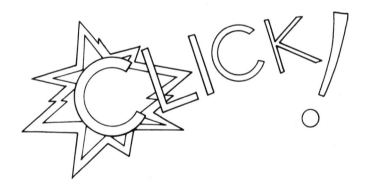

"Any more questions?" Dame Honey grinned, as the fairies all chattered at each other and scribbled notes on their petal pads.

"What kind of beetle is Pipsqueak, Dame Honey?" Tiptoe asked.

"A Rainbow Leaf Beetle," said Dame Honey, holding aside a fern frond so that the fairies could walk underneath it. "They're quite rare."

"Where do you think Pipsqueak is, Dame Honey?" Sesame asked.

Dame Honey looked serious. "I don't know, Sesame," she said. "I wish I did."

"What do Rainbow Leaf Beetles eat?" Nettle asked.

"Mostly wild thyme," said Dame Honey. "It doesn't grow in this Hedge."

"Naughty Fairies!" Tiptoe squeaked breathlessly, as Dame Honey pushed deeper into the Hedge.

"Nit flippers."

"Numb fingers."

"Nuts first."

"Gnat fat!"

"Gnat starts with a 'g', Sesame," Brilliance sighed. Sesame wasn't very good at spelling. "Nodule flake. What is it, Tiptoe?"

"I smelt some wild thyme in the Wood yesterday!" Tiptoe said. "If I have to go to the Wood on another fetching job for Turnip tonight, you could come with me and get the thyme! I'd, er – I don't want to go on my own again," she added, feeling a bit lame.

"Because of those dark things, I suppose," said Nettle. "OK, we'll come. We'll hang around outside the kitchen doors tonight. Come out and tell us if Turnip says anything about sending you out again."

"Thanks," Tiptoe said happily. "You guys are the best."

Tiptoe washed up the plates as quickly as she could that night. Turnip gave her three acorn cups of mush to give to the school maggots in their pen.

Shuddering a bit, Tiptoe emptied the

acorn cups among the wriggling white bodies, trying not to look at the maggots' munching jaws.

Back in the kitchen, a delicious smell wafted up Tiptoe's nose. She stopped in her tracks."Toffee!" she said, before she could stop herself.

"Aye, toffee," said Turnip, looking round from the large pot he was stirring. "We always finish the May Day Feast with my special recipe."

Tiptoe could feel her taste buds jumping around in her mouth. The toffee smelt so delicious – so nutty – so . . . She sniffed. The extra *something* wasn't there.

Turnip muttered something to himself. Frowning, he looked on the shelves standing either side of the firefly where the toffee pot was boiling. "I canna be out of it," he growled in annoyance.

"Out of what, sir?" Tiptoe asked.

"Marsh thistle," said Turnip absently.

"I've just enough for this batch, but I'll
need to make more tomorrow morning.
I'll have to send ye on another fetching
job. Caddy knows the place." He put
his fingers in his mouth and whistled.
Tiptoe heard Caddy rubbing his legs
together outside the kitchen door.

Tiptoe's head was in a whirl. Marsh thistle. The secret ingredient!

*Turnip had just told her his toffee's secret ingredient!*

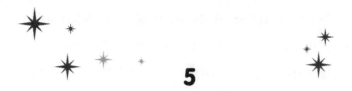

# 5

# Night Sprites

"For someone on detention, you look very pleased with yourself," said Nettle.

Tiptoe's friends were waiting for her around the back of the kitchen flowerpot, as planned.

Tiptoe grinned from high up on Caddy's back. "I've got to go and fetch . . . something," she said. "Is everyone ready?"

"It's too far to fly on our own," Brilliance said. "We have to go and get some butterflies."

"And Pong," Ping said immediately.

"And Flea," Kelpie said. "He's still eating honeycake crumbs off the Dining Flowerpot floor."

"So we have to go and get some butterflies, and Ping's dragonfly, and Kelpie's bee," Brilliance sighed, rolling her eyes. "We'll follow you as soon as we can."

"Meet me at the big hawthorn at the edge of the Wood," Tiptoe said, tugging on Caddy's reins as the grasshopper flapped his wings impatiently. "Don't be long!" she called over her shoulder, as Caddy leaped towards the Hedge.

It was easier to stay on Caddy's back this time. Tiptoe held lightly on to his reins, and thought happily about toffee all the way across the Meadow. Marsh thistle! She'd never have guessed from the way the toffee tasted. Now that she knew the secret ingredient she could make the toffee for herself.

Suddenly Tiptoe realised that they were leaping deep into the Wood. She'd forgotten to steer Caddy to the hawthorn tree. She tugged hard on

Caddy's reins, but the grasshopper leaped steadily on.

"Turn . . . around!" Tiptoe panted, heaving on the reins. Caddy shook his head crossly and did a twisting half leap over a twig that was lying on the path. Taken by surprise, Tiptoe fell off and banged her head hard on the muddy ground.

Everything went black.

Swimming up from a broken, confused dream of grasshoppers with soft black wings, Tiptoe opened her eyes. She winced, and felt the back of her head. There was a lump behind her earlobe and a whining sound deep in her left ear.

"Caddy?" Tiptoe called, rubbing her head. Her voice echoed through the gloomy Wood. She frowned uneasily. When did it suddenly get so dark?

"Caddy?" she said again. "Where have you gone?"

The wind rustled at some leaves nearby, making Tiptoe jump. It really was dark. How long had she been lying here? Her heart began to beat faster. She stood up and looked around.

There was no moon tonight. The trees were black and the night was black and the ground was black. There was no sign of Caddy.

She was lost.

Tiptoe felt tears welling in her eyes. She bit her lip, determined not to cry. Unfurling her wings, she flew up in the air and hovered uncertainly. Which way should she go?

A light was glimmering through the trees. Perhaps it was Ambrosia Academy. Although Tiptoe didn't want to meet the Ambrosia fairies again, at least Ambrosia Academy was on the edge of the Wood. She'd be able to find the Meadow from there. Trying not to think about crossing the Meadow and

passing through the Hedge in the
moonless night, Tiptoe angled her
wings and headed for the glimmer. She
called Caddy's name. Then she called
the names of her friends.

*Caddy . . . dy . . . dy . . . ! Sesame . . .
me . . . me . . . !*

Her voice echoed off the trees. Tiptoe

flew as fast as she dared in the darkness towards the light.

The glimmer took on a greenish tinge. This wasn't Ambrosia Academy at all. It was just a cluster of glow worms, wriggling on the ground in a dark, damp-smelling glade. Feeling sick with fear, Tiptoe recognised the smell. It was the marsh mud she'd smelled the night before, when she'd seen . . .

*Whoosh.*

As light as a feather, something soft and dark whispered past her. Then another – and another. Soon there were four or five, whisking along in a dark blur. By the light of the glow worms, Tiptoe saw what looked like black cobwebs twirling in the air – and then, to her shock, a pale green face appeared in front of her.

Tiptoe gaped. The green face grinned at her, and whisked out of view again. It had been riding a hairy black moth

with mottled wings. But what was it? It wasn't a fairy. Imps didn't fly on moths. The only things that flew on moths were . . . *Night sprites.*

Tiptoe sat down suddenly. She'd heard of night sprites in stories. But she'd never seen one. She didn't know

anyone who had. But here they were,
plain as – well, not day exactly, but . . .

Clusters of night sprites were
swooping down on the glow worms,
then banking sharply up again and
spinning around in the night. They
seemed to be racing each other. Tiptoe
could hear a very faint chittering, like
the sound of bats, as they whisked
along, their cobweb cloaks flapping

silently behind them.

"Excuse me?" she said. Her voice sounded thin and scared. "I need to get out of the Wood. I've got to find Caddy, and find some marsh thistle, and can you – please can you tell me the way out of here?"

The night sprites all stopped dead, hovering in mid-air like a shoal of airborne fish. Then they darted off again through a dark patch of trees. With nothing better to do, Tiptoe whirred her wings and followed.

Following the night sprites was almost impossible. They stopped and started and changed direction so often that Tiptoe kept losing them. Doggedly she flew on, hoping and hoping that they'd reach the edge of the Wood soon.

The smell of marsh mud reached her nostrils, stronger and wetter than before. With mounting despair, Tiptoe realised that they were even deeper in the Wood than before.

Night sprites spun around her, making her dizzy. With one last exhausted flap, she landed on the ground and fell to her knees. Then, just as suddenly as they'd appeared, they had gone.

Silence.

Tiptoe stared at the deep, quiet darkness around her with terrified eyes.

Then she wrapped her arms around her
knees and started to cry. The night
sprites had tricked her, and now she

was lost for ever . . . lost . . . lost . . .

"What a stink," came Kelpie's voice. "Did you just fart, Sesame?"

Tiptoe shut her eyes and clamped her hands to her ears. The sprites were pretending to be her friends now, tricking her into hoping . . .

"Of course I didn't! It's the marsh gas you idiot."

Tiptoe moaned and huddled down in the darkness. *Please make them go away*, she begged silently. *Please . . .*

"There she is!" Nettle said. "Tiptoe, why are you sitting in a puddle?"

"You're totally ruining your dress," said Brilliance disapprovingly.

Tiptoe looked up in disbelief. The dark glade had taken on a greenish glow. Hovering in the air above her were five figures sitting on a large dragonfly. The dragonfly had some kind of light on its head.

Ping peered down at Tiptoe. "Pong

took some persuading to come out in the dark," she said cheerfully, "but then Sesame thought of tying on Flash like a headlamp. Good, huh?"

## 6

# Toffee

"Sorry we're late," said Nettle, slipping off Pong's back. "The butterflies were asleep, and Flea was just – well, totally useless to be honest . . . "

"Hey!" Kelpie said indignantly.

"So we just had Pong, who doesn't like the dark, and you know the rest," Nettle finished. She looked at Tiptoe. "Are you OK?"

Tiptoe burst into tears. "How did you find me?" she sniffed at last.

"Easy," said Brilliance. "We asked Turnip what he'd sent you out for."

"He told you about . . . the secret ingredient?" Tiptoe asked feeling rather surprised.

"He told us about the marsh thistle," Nettle said, nodding. "So after we didn't find you at the hawthorn, we looked for marshy ground in the Wood. And here we are."

"I didn't realise this was the marsh," Tiptoe mumbled, dashing the tears from her eyes.

"Duh," said Kelpie. "Smell that! This isn't a rose bed."

The wet, pungent smell hit Tiptoe's nostrils again. "Maybe the night sprites didn't trick me after all," she whispered, almost to herself. "In the end, they led me to my friends."

The others burst out laughing.

"Night sprites!" Brilliance giggled. "Those ghost stories last night really worked on you, didn't they Tiptoe? Come on. Let's find this oh-so-special marsh thistle and get out of here. This place seriously honks."

*

With the marsh thistle strapped to Pong's sides, the fairies flew back to St Juniper's. Tiptoe twisted her head and sniffed. "I can smell thyme," she said, as Pong swooped over the Meadow and into the Hedge Tunnel. "Did you find some, then?"

"Loads," said Sesame, patting the woven grass bag on her back. "It's all safely in here."

Pong dropped down to the butterfly stables and came to rest on the ground. Sesame carefully untied Flash.

"Better let Flash go," said Brilliance.

Sesame looked upset. "Do I have to?"

"Not if you don't want to," Nettle said kindly.

"But Dame Lacewing will give you a detention if you don't," Kelpie added. "Remember what she said last night?"

Sesame cuddled Flash for a moment. Then she put her down. The glow worm wiggled off into the dark, until her

flashing tail could no longer be seen.

"We can put some wild thyme out for Pipsqueak before we go to bed," said Tiptoe, putting her arm round Sesame. "That'll take your mind off Flash."

"Who's going to bed?" Brilliance asked, with a gleam in her eye. "Naughty Fairies!"

"Neurotic flimflam!" said Ping, rubbing down Pong's scales and putting him in his stable.

Full of high spirits after their

adventure in the Wood, the other fairies wasted no time.

"Nice feet!"

"Nervous fruitfly!"

"Night flight!"

"Nostril fuel! What's the plan, Brilliance?"

"Food," Brilliance whispered. "Lots of lovely May Day food, just waiting for hungry fairies to find . . . "

The Kitchen Flowerpot was dark. It looked like Turnip had packed up for the night. Caddy the grasshopper was standing by the kitchen door, his head hanging down.

"This is all your fault," Tiptoe began.

"Don't scold him, Tiptoe," Sesame begged. "He probably got scared too."

Tiptoe took the baskets off Caddy's back and tethered the grasshopper by the door. Then, cautiously, she pushed the door open. The hungry fairies walked into the warm, scented kitchen with glazed eyes.

"We've been here before," Nettle warned. "Let's not knock anything over this time, OK?"

"Mmm," Brilliance sighed. "I can smell harebell hearts!"

"And sugared buttercups," Sesame murmured, trailing her fingers over the box of stiff yellow petals. "And buckthorn pasties, and sorrel custard . . . "

"Mint twists . . . "

"Cornflower crepes . . . "

"And toffee," Tiptoe whispered, staring down at the tray of toffee in front of her. "Lovely, lovely toffee!"

"Nobody finish anything," Ping advised. "That way, Turnip won't notice a thing."

The fairies fell on the food with delight. A mint twist here – a sugared buttercup there. Everything tasted nicer for being eaten in the dark.

"Pass the toffee, Tiptoe," Brilliance mumbled, her mouth full of jasmine pie.

Tiptoe's tummy felt so full that she could hardly move. She reached up for the toffee tray. "It's empty," she said.

"Shame," Nettle murmured.

Tiptoe's eyes suddenly pinged open. Empty! They'd eaten all the toffee!

"Problem!" she gasped. "We have a big, big problem!"

Turnip might not notice the odd

cornflower crepe had gone missing, or
one or two buckthorn pasties. But a
whole tray of toffee?

"We always finish the May Day feast
with toffee," Nettle said in dismay.

Tiptoe got to her feet. "Don't panic,"
she said, as firmly as she could. "We'll
just have to make some more. I know
how to do it. I watched Turnip tonight."

"But the secret ingredient—"
Sesame began.

"Marsh thistle, remember?" Tiptoe's head suddenly felt very clear. "Start chopping the thistle, Nettle," she instructed. "Wash off those disgusting black bugs first. Ping, weigh the honey crystals and the nut flakes. Turnip won't even notice the difference."

The fairies started chopping and weighing, stirring and measuring. Tiptoe adjusted the firefly and boiled the honey crystals, lavender petals, nut flakes and marsh thistle. Soon the toffee pot was blopping quietly and scenting the room with its sweetness.

"It smells different," Sesame said, as they poured the toffee into the waiting toffee tray.

"That's just because it's hot," said Tiptoe, scraping out the last of the toffee from the bottom of the pot. She was dying to try it, but she didn't want to burn her mouth.

Leaving the toffee to set, the fairies

rearranged the May Day Feast food to cover the gaps. They washed up the toffee things, and put the ingredients carefully back on the shelves. Then they crept out, full and happy, scattered wild thyme around the courtyard to tempt Pipsqueak out of hiding, and headed for their soft foxglove beds.

May Day morning dawned bright and warm. Fairies swarmed out of the dormitories and into the dawn-lit sports field, where breakfast had been laid out on pale rose petal rugs.

"Fresh clover buns," Tiptoe said in ecstasy. "They're the best."

"I don't know how you can eat after last night," Brilliance sighed, pushing her rose-hip toast to one side.

"New day, new food," Tiptoe grinned.

After breakfast, Dame Fuddle announced the order of events. There was maypole dancing around a twig festooned with grass ribbons at one end of the Sports Field. There was also fairy ring dancing on the circle of dark grass by the Hedge Tunnel, which Bindweed the garden pixie had been preparing all week. Butterfly cricket would follow lunch, and then there would be a performance of fairy favourites by the St Juniper's school choir.

"Look!" Sesame gasped as they made their way to the maypole twig. "Pipsqueak's back!"

Dame Lacewing strode past them, deep in conversation with Dame Taffeta. Bustling along beside her was Pipsqueak, his pink and green wing cases gleaming in the sun. There was a trail of wild thyme peeping out of his mouth. He glanced nervously at the Naughty Fairies, and pressed close to Dame Lacewing's ankles as they passed by.

"Looks like he hasn't forgotten your Flea threat," Nettle said.

Kelpie grinned. "Could be very useful," she said.

"Pipsqueak coming back makes everything perfect," said Tiptoe happily, picking up a grass ribbon for the maypole dancing. She did a little pirouette. "Just perfect . . . oops. Sorry. Tangled up a bit there. Are you OK, Ping?"

Soon the maypole was wrapped up tightly in its grass ribbons, together with three small weeping fairies who'd managed to get wrapped up as well. The Naughty Fairies trailed over to try their luck at the fairy ring dance. This was quite complicated, and involved snaking hand movements and weaving around in a chain. The fairies ended up in even more of a knot than they had at the maypole, but this time it involved arms and legs rather than grass and proved a bit more painful.

"Butterfly cricket will commence after lunch, in precisely one dandelion," Dame Fuddle announced, mopping her forehead with a petal handkerchief.

The fairies cheered, and rushed back to the petal rugs. This time, a huge

lunch had been laid out along a bark table, with leaf plates, cutlery and petal napkins stacked at either end. The fairies carried their food back to the rugs and fell on it like they hadn't eaten for weeks.

"I wish it could be the May Day Feast every day of the year," Tiptoe sighed, sinking her teeth into a delicious buckthorn pasty.

"Flea would get fat," said Kelpie, patting her bumblebee. Flea lay snoring on the rug, a scattering of sugared buttercups and honeycake crumbs around him.

"He's already fat," Nettle said, taking a long drink of elderflower fizz.

Arguing happily, the fairies finished their plates and went up to the bark table for a slice of Turnip's nut meringue and, at last – a piece of toffee.

"Let's see what this toffee's like, then," said Brilliance, settling down on the petal rug and taking a bite.

"It looks OK," said Sesame, helping herself to a piece and holding it up to the light.

Tiptoe lifted the toffee to her lips. It *almost* smelled right, she thought to herself. Perhaps she should have boiled it a little longer.

"Toot," said Brilliance.

"Nice whistle, Brilliance," Tiptoe said, about to put the toffee in her mouth.

"Toot toot."

Sesame also started whistling. Then Nettle. Tiptoe put her toffee down. "Is this a game?" she asked in excitement. "Ooh, what are the rules?"

The whistling was spreading across the Sports Field. Fewer and fewer fairy voices could be heard. Fairies began to get up from their picnic rugs and clutch their throats.

"You're not doing this on purpose . . . are you?" Tiptoe said in a small voice, staring at her friends.

Her friends shook their heads mutely, their eyes wide and anxious. Flea licked a piece of toffee and gave a shrill bee whistle, before zooming into the sky in a whirl of terror.

There was sudden pandemonium. Little fairies rushed past the Naughty

Fairies' picnic rug, sobbing in broken, whispery whistles. Leaf plates were upended, kicked over by panicking fairy feet. One small group of fairies were making the best of the situation by whistling together in close harmony.

Meanwhile, over at the staff picnic rug, Dame Fuddle was running around in circles. "Wheee!" she tooted in desperation. "Peeee! Flee whee!"

"Parp," Lord Gallivant added. He
looked appalled.

Behind Lord Gallivant's back,
Bindweed slyly flapped his hand in
front of his face and pulled a face. Dame
Honey and Dame Taffeta collapsed in
shrill whistly giggles, which then
seemed to make them giggle even
harder. Around Bindweed's feet, the
leaf-cutting ants were standing among

crumbs of toffee and peeping at each
other in impossibly high voices.

"Tootle tink tonk toot . . . " Only
Dame Lacewing could make a whistle
sound menacing, thought Tiptoe

nervously, as the teacher glared around the field for the culprits.

Turnip came storming across the Sports Field towards Tiptoe. She sat frozen to the spot. The kitchen pixie's face was crimson with rage.

"Ye daft fairy fool!" Turnip roared. "Ye tried to make the toffee, didn't ye? *Didn't* ye?"

# 7

# Bugs

"How was I to know?" Tiptoe protested, standing at the Kitchen Flowerpot door later that evening. "I thought they were just bugs!"

Kelpie prodded Tiptoe with a menacing finger. "I had to drink bug juice," she said. *"Bug juice*! Do you know what that tastes like?"

"Sort of . . . black and slimy?" Tiptoe ventured weakly.

Brilliance made a gagging noise. "Don't say the 's' word," she moaned, holding her stomach.

*"The secret ingredient's marsh thistle, remember?"* Sesame mimicked Tiptoe's

voice. "How could you, Tiptoe?"

"I can't believe you didn't have to drink that stuff," said Ping, shaking her head in amazement.

"How come you didn't eat the toffee?" Nettle asked.

"I just didn't get round to it," Tiptoe said. "Listen, I'm really sorry. I didn't know you had to use the thistle *and* the thistle bugs. I'm in detention for the next hundred years. What more do you want?"

"On the subject of detentions," said Turnip, coming up behind Tiptoe with a scary smile on his face, "I've a wee maggot-related task for ye."

"Got to go," Tiptoe said, swallowing. "See you later."

She left her friends standing at the kitchen door and followed Turnip meekly to the maggots' enclosure.

"By the time I've finished with ye, young fairy," Turnip growled, "ye'll never want another bite of toffee in

yer life. D'ye hear me?"

Tiptoe thought of Turnip's slimy, six-legged secret ingredient. Somehow, she didn't think she'd miss it.

*Also available from*
*Hodder Children's Books*

# Bumble Rumble

Kelpie's bumblebee is so furry that you can't see his knees – he's bound to win the Furriest Bumblebee trophy. But enter a pathetic competition like that – what about Kelpie's Hedge cred?

Still, if it's about beating Ambrosia Academy it will be worth it!